Oliver
The Ornament™

Written by Todd M. Zimmermann

Illustrated by Teddy Lu

This book is dedicated to Marlene and Ted Zimmermann, and Joan and Norb Hoerst, for providing your families with loving homes, filled with magic and creativity at Christmas and throughout the year. And for inspiring your children to accomplish anything they dream possible.

For John

OLIVER'S AMBASSADORS

This special group of family and friends are helping to spread the word of this heartwarming tale.

Kelly Arst

Beth Markus-Boles and Anthony Boles

Julie and Joe Bower

Kelly and Jack Francis

Audrea Fulton

Nori and Teddy Greenstein

Jodi and Steve Heim

Bridget and Brian Hoffman

Tom and Denise Kazar

Bob Malenchini and Nick Maviano

Sally and Jody Moulton

Rachel and Mark Noltner

Kelly and Tom Rieckelman

Kathy Sanville

Nancy and Don Schacher

Loreen Strasser

Ann and Bill Sutmar

Marlene Zimmermann

WITH SPECIAL THANKS TO

John Hoerst, Marlene Zimmermann, and Joan Hoerst

Thanks also to Kelly Arst, The Bower Family (especially Lauren and Jack), The Cattau Family (especially Ava), The Durrett Family (especially Sarah and Carley), Dusty and Joyce Eling, Jessica Eling, The Francis Family (especially Jack, Emma, and Will), The Greenstein Family (especially Elle and Emmy), Gary Gronlund, Nancy and Jack Hanson, Eric Hirsh, Becky Hoerst, Denny and Maggie Hoerst, Fred and Loretta Hoerst, Tim and Joyce Hoerst, Diana Laskaris, Bob Malenchini, The McCue Family (especially Declan and Emmett), Kelly McNees, Nick Maviano, Sue and Fred Mendell, The Moulton Family (especially Avery and Jackson), The Noltner Family (especially Siena), Tom O'Reilly, Rose and Ron Ostermann, Sue Reddel, Marcia and Dave Reuscher, The Rieckelman Family (especially Haley and Austin), Karen and Dave Stevenson, Ann Sutmar, Tom Trucco, The Urquhart Family (especially Quinn and Fallon), Gary Zimmermann, Mark Zimmermann and Carole Kaspryzcki

The smell of Thanksgiving dinner was still in the air. The guests had gone home hours ago, and now it was time for Henry and Holly to go to bed. Tomorrow was going to be a big day. Tomorrow, they were going to decorate their Christmas tree.

Mom and Dad tucked both of them in, and then went to bed themselves. Soon, the whole family was in dreamland.

But not everyone in the Nelson household was dreaming. Oh no, not at all. In fact, some were just getting up. Getting up from a very, very long nap.

You see, packed away deep in the Nelson attic were many boxes filled with some of the family's most precious possessions. These boxes were filled with their cherished Christmas ornaments.

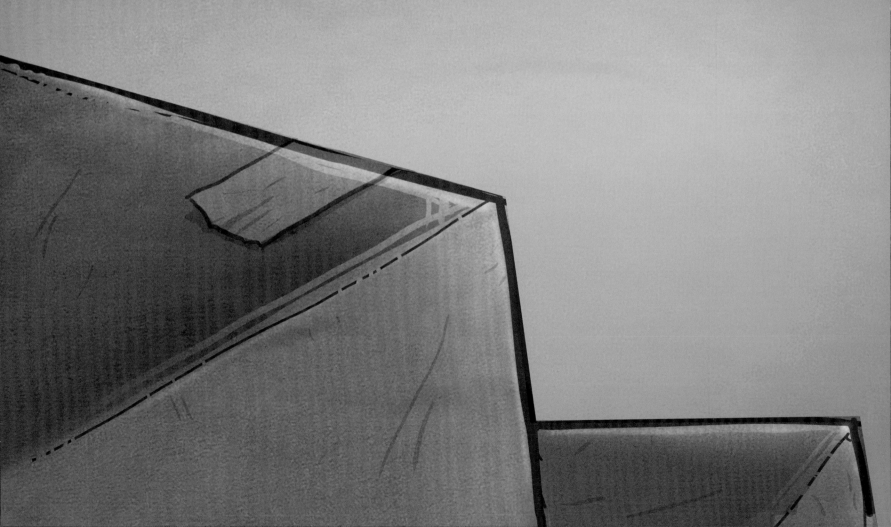

There was Belle,  a very cute little bell. And Abbey,

a sweet church. There was Norb,  a German singer,

and Teddy, an adorable bear. There was Buck,

a lovable old moose, and Edsel, a fiery fire truck.

There was Crystal,  a dazzling snowflake, and

Frasier, a glorious Christmas tree. There was Merry,

a bright and shiny wreath, and, for the top of the tree, there

was a pair of beautiful angels named  Marley and Joan.

The most special of all the ornaments, though, was Oliver,

a little boy who was the Nelsons' very first Christmas ornament.

"Hey, Oliver — wake up. It's time to get ready. Tomorrow is our big day," said Belle.

"Oh, Belle, is it that time already?" Oliver asked in a sleepy voice as he rubbed his eyes. "You sure look nice," he added.

Belle liked Oliver because he often said nice things to her and the other ornaments.

Suddenly, Edsel zoomed by with his red lights flashing and siren screaming.

"Whoa, slow down, Edsel! You'll run someone over!" Oliver shouted as he jumped out of the way.

"Don't tell me to slow down — you're useless!" Edsel replied.

One by one, the Nelson ornaments were rising from their three-season sleep. They danced, they sang, but most of all they cleaned themselves off for the big day ahead of them.

"What happened to your arm, Oliver?" Belle asked.

"Oh, it broke this summer, but it's okay," Oliver said. "It doesn't hurt too much. It just kind of looks funny."

"Ha, now you can't do anything that the rest of us can do," shouted Edsel.

"You're useless," he teased.

"I am *not* useless. I can do a lot of things," replied Oliver.

"Oh, yeah? Like what?" chimed in Buck.

"Well, I can—umm...well, I can..." Oliver tried to stick up for himself, but he just couldn't find the right words.

"Like I said, Oliver is useless," Edsel laughed again.

Marley stuck up for Oliver, saying, "If you don't have something nice to say, you shouldn't say anything at all, Edsel."

But, sadly, some of the other ornaments joined in

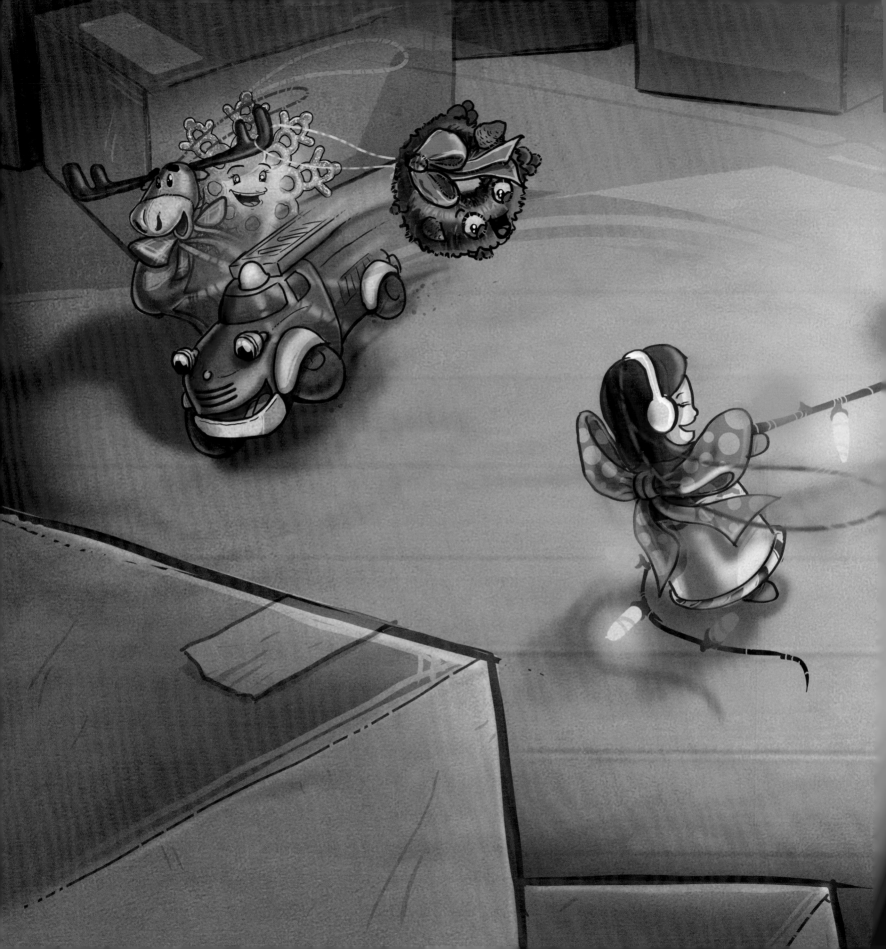

After the bullying of Oliver ended, the ornaments continued playing and dancing and shining themselves up for tomorrow's big day. Then, one by one, they hopped back in their boxes to get a good night's sleep.

When all the ornaments were in their boxes, Edsel hopped back out and quietly tapped on Buck's box.

"What's up, Edsel?" asked Buck.

Edsel whispered back, "Hey, let's play a trick on Oliver."

"Oh, let's just leave him alone," replied Buck.

Edsel insisted, and Buck gave in, so they hid Oliver's box behind the Easter baskets, where no one could see it. Oliver knew something was going on, but Buck and Edsel had taped his box shut, so he couldn't open the top.

"It's okay," Oliver told himself. "The Nelsons will come get me tomorrow. I just can't wait to see them. I love them so much." With those happy thoughts, he went to sleep.

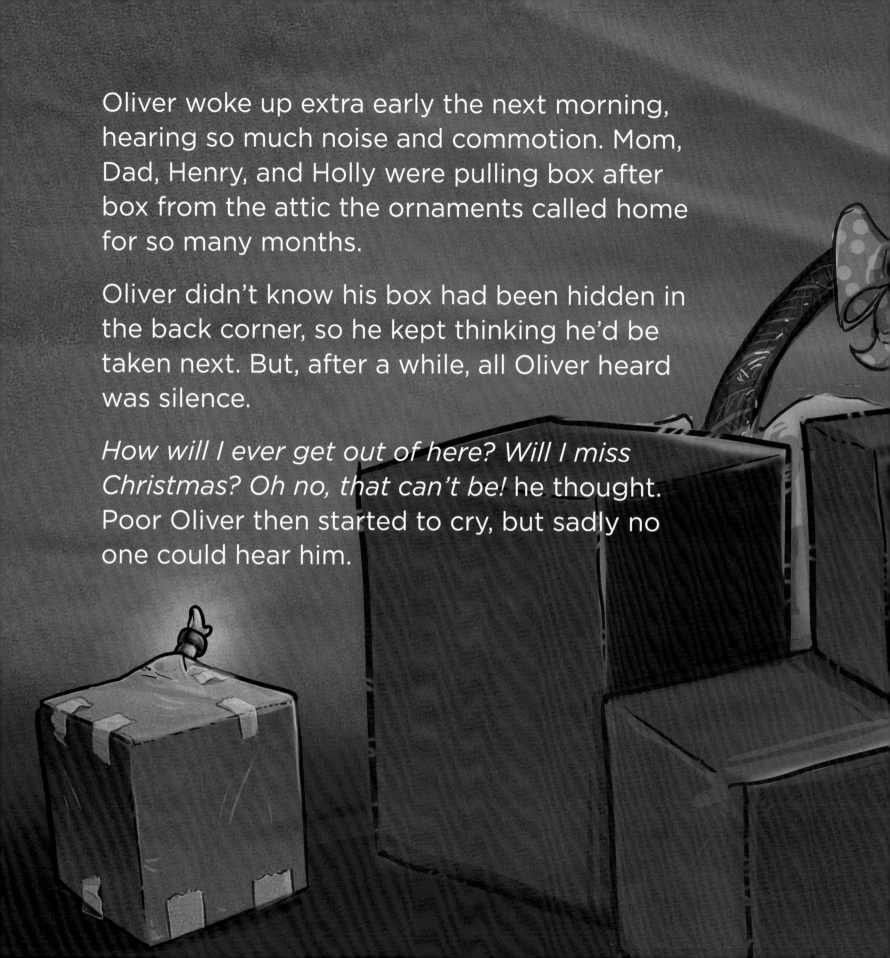

Oliver woke up extra early the next morning, hearing so much noise and commotion. Mom, Dad, Henry, and Holly were pulling box after box from the attic the ornaments called home for so many months.

Oliver didn't know his box had been hidden in the back corner, so he kept thinking he'd be taken next. But, after a while, all Oliver heard was silence.

How will I ever get out of here? Will I miss Christmas? Oh no, that can't be! he thought. Poor Oliver then started to cry, but sadly no one could hear him.

Meanwhile, Mom, Dad, Henry, and Holly were busy hanging the ornaments on the tree. You could see the excitement on each ornament's face as it found its new home on this beautiful Christmas tree.

When the tree was completely decorated, Mom wondered what had happened to Oliver. *He'll turn up at some point. He just has to,* she thought.

Once the Nelson family left the room, Belle asked Edsel, "What did you do to Oliver?"

"Nothing. I don't know anything," said Edsel.

"Come on, Edsel. Oliver was the first ornament ever on the tree," pleaded Frasier.

"What's the big deal?" said Crystal. "He's so old, and he's useless."

Teddy and Norb disagreed and shouted so all the ornaments could hear, "We have to find Oliver!"

That evening, Mom and Dad went out for dinner. When the babysitter arrived, she asked Henry and Holly to help clean up by putting the ornament boxes into the attic. Henry and Holly did as they were asked.

As they approached the attic, they heard crying from inside. It sounded like the crying was coming from a box behind the Easter baskets. Henry and Holly opened the box and saw Oliver, but he didn't want them to see him cry, so he pretended to be asleep. Henry and Holly then closed the box, thinking that Mom and Dad didn't want to hang Oliver up this year — he did, after all, have a broken arm.

As they walked away, they heard crying again. They returned to the box but once again saw a very still Oliver. This continued several more times, until they opened the box and heard Oliver sneeze.

"God bless you," said the children.

"Thank you," replied Oliver.

Henry and Holly were amazed, and Oliver was bewildered. He realized his cover was blown. After all, ornaments aren't supposed to be able to talk.

"Who are you?" asked Holly.

Oliver answered, "Close your eyes and start to imagine your Mom and Dad years ago.

"You see," he continued, "it was on their very first date. They were ice skating in the town square just before Christmas. I could see them from the window in the Village Shoppe where I was hanging. They then came into the shop, and your Dad bought me for your Mom. I think he bought me because my skates were just like his. Later, he gave me to her as he said good night.

When she got home, she hung me on her tree. I was the only ornament on the tree at that time. From the smile on your Mom's face, I knew right then and there that they were perfect for each other — and that they would be together forever."

Holly and Henry loved Oliver immediately, and they insisted he come down and claim his place on the tree. Oliver didn't think Mom and Dad wanted him on the tree, so he didn't want to go. But after some convincing, he agreed.

As they walked down the stairs, all the ornaments, except Edsel, Buck, and Crystal, got very excited to finally see Oliver.

"Tell us more stories, Oliver," said Henry.

So Oliver started telling the stories of the family. Like when Mom and Dad got engaged under their Christmas tree, and when they got married, and when Mom and Dad brought both Henry and Holly home from the hospital after they were born.

Oliver told them stories of family gatherings, and more good times than you could ever imagine.

Then Oliver told them stories about all the different ornaments. One by one, he called out his friends on the tree, telling their stories, and how each of them was so very special to Mom and Dad.

Like the fire truck ornament that was given to their parents when Henry was born, or the angels and church that were given to them to look out for a sick little girl, Oliver told them. Henry and Holly's eyes glowed with amazement and wonder.

"You see, Henry and Holly," said Oliver, "Every Ornament Tells a Story."

As he said this, Crystal started melting from her eyes, and tears started to roll down Edsel's headlights. And Buck — well, Buck was so upset he couldn't stop crying. He felt so bad about how he had treated Oliver.

The babysitter came in and told Henry and Holly that it was time for them to go to bed. Henry and Holly kissed Oliver and told him that he was going on the tree.

"Only if you put me on the *back* of the tree," Oliver pleaded. "I don't think your Mom and Dad wanted me on the tree this year."

Henry and Holly disagreed, telling Oliver it was a misunderstanding, but they respected his wishes and placed him on the back of the tree. As they did, Oliver looked back at his new friends and winked at both of them.

Once the children were upstairs and the brightly lit tree sat alone, Belle said, "Well, what do you have to say for yourself, Edsel?"

"Oh, Oliver, I'm sorry. I guess I'm just…well, gee… I sure am sorry. I really liked hearing all your stories," Edsel replied.

Merry and Abbey added, "What about you, Crystal?"

She quickly responded, saying, "If I cry anymore, I'll be a snowball instead of a snowflake. Oliver, I'm so sorry."

"No worries," said Oliver. "We're all here, and we're all going to help the Nelsons have the best Christmas ever."

Then Edsel said, "You know, Oliver, I'm in your place. You should be right here in the front of the tree."

But everyone else said, "No, Edsel, you can't move yourself. Only people can move you."

"I'm a fire truck, so I think I can handle it," he insisted. "Oliver, this is your spot."

So Edsel unhooked his ladder from the tree and jumped to the next branch, but disaster struck. Edsel was falling off the tree, hitting one branch after another, until he was almost to the floor, where he would surely shatter into a thousand pieces.

The ornaments all screamed, "Oh, no!"

Then, out of nowhere, Oliver swooped down and caught Edsel using his good arm. Edsel couldn't believe it. Oliver had swung, jumped, skated, and climbed down to save him!

Oliver climbed back up the tree, carrying Edsel, and placed him in the front of the tree. Then he went back to his spot where Henry and Holly had placed him. All the ornaments cheered Oliver.

Joan yelled out from the top of the tree, "Keep up the good work, Oliver!" while the others all proclaimed, "You're a hero, Oliver."

An embarrassed Oliver began to blush.

Just then, Mom and Dad came home and said good-bye to the babysitter. As they sat in front of the tree, Mom said, "You know, I couldn't find Oliver today. He was our first ornament, and he's been with us since our first date. I'll have to find him tomorrow because it just wouldn't be Christmas without him. I love that little guy so much."

Oliver heard this and got a big smile on his face and a tear in his eye. Dad looked toward the back of the tree and saw something glittering. As he looked closer, he realized it was coming from Oliver — what Dad saw was actually Oliver's tear of happiness.

"Hey, Mom, look — you did bring Oliver out!" said Dad.

"No, I didn't. It must have been Henry or Holly," she replied. "But one thing's for sure: Oliver belongs on the front of the tree."

Then Mom realized that Oliver's arm was broken.

"Oh, no — this can't be. I'll just have to fix this," she said.

So she got a Christmas napkin and made a sling for Oliver's arm and placed it on him, making everything better for Oliver.

And then Mom and Dad hung Oliver right in the front of the tree just above Edsel, surrounded by Belle, Teddy, Abbey, Norb, Crystal, and the rest of his friends.

Mom and Dad turned off the lights on the tree and went to bed, but then the magic of Christmas lit the tree up again, and all the ornaments sang together.

Oliver felt the Christmas spirit more than ever, knowing how much his family and friends loved him, and how much he loved them in return.

The next morning, Mom and Dad woke up Henry and Holly and brought them down to the tree. They told them that today they were going to hear about each of the ornaments on the tree and the stories that made them so very special.

When Henry and Holly looked up, they saw that Oliver was on the front of the tree, with his repaired arm in a sling.

"Let's start with the first one," said Dad. "His name is Oliver." Henry and Holly looked at Oliver, and when Mom and Dad weren't looking, Oliver winked at them both.

"We found this special guy on our very first date," continued Dad. And with that began Mom and Dad's story of each of their cherished Christmas ornaments.

And so dear friends, as you hang me on your tree this year, look around at all of your beautiful ornaments. Sit down in front of the tree with your family, and have them tell you the stories of the ornaments next to me. You never know — there just might be another Oliver on your own Christmas tree. Because, after all, Every Ornament Tells a Story. Like the time I met Belle...

Love,

Oliver

Oliver & Friends, Inc.
P.O. Box 13304
Chicago, IL   60613

olivertheornament.com

ISBN 978-0-9863416-2-5

Printed in China.

Every Ornament Tells a Story™

Here's A Place For You To Tell Yours

_____

_____

_____

_____

_____

_____

_____

_____

_____

_____

Every Ornament Tells a Story™

Here's A Place For You To Tell Yours

_____

_____

_____

_____

_____

_____

_____

_____

_____

_____

_____

Every Ornament Tells a Story™

Here's A Place For You To Tell Yours

_____

_____

_____

_____

_____

_____

_____

_____

_____

_____

_____

Every Ornament Tells a Story™

Here's A Place For You To Tell Yours

_____

_____

_____

_____

_____

_____

_____

_____

_____

_____

_____